THE MYSTERY OF THE HIDDEN PAINTING
created by
GERTRUDE CHANDLER WARNER

Illustrated by Charles Tang

ALBERT WHITMAN & Company
Morton Grove, Illinois

Library of Congress Cataloging-in-Publication Data
Warner, Gertrude Chandler, 1890-1979.
The mystery of the hidden painting /
created by Gertrude Chandler Warner ;
illustrated by Charles Tang.
p.   cm.
Summary: The Alden children hunt for their
late grandmother's necklace that has been
missing for years.
ISBN 0-8075-5383-2. —ISBN 0-8075-5379-4
(pbk.)
[1. Mystery and detective stories.]   I. Tang,
Charles, ill.   II. Title.
PZ7.W244Mx   1992
[Fic]—dc20   91-33846
                                                    CIP
                                                    AC

Cover art by David Cunningham.

The Boxcar Children® Mysteries

THE BOXCAR CHILDREN
SURPRISE ISLAND
THE YELLOW HOUSE MYSTERY
MYSTERY RANCH
MIKE'S MYSTERY
BLUE BAY MYSTERY
THE WOODSHED MYSTERY
THE LIGHTHOUSE MYSTERY
MOUNTAIN TOP MYSTERY
SCHOOLHOUSE MYSTERY
CABOOSE MYSTERY
HOUSEBOAT MYSTERY
SNOWBOUND MYSTERY
TREE HOUSE MYSTERY
BICYCLE MYSTERY
MYSTERY IN THE SAND
MYSTERY BEHIND THE WALL
BUS STATION MYSTERY
BENNY UNCOVERS A MYSTERY
THE HAUNTED CABIN MYSTERY
THE DESERTED LIBRARY MYSTERY
THE ANIMAL SHELTER MYSTERY
THE OLD MOTEL MYSTERY
THE MYSTERY OF THE HIDDEN PAINTING
THE AMUSEMENT PARK MYSTERY
THE MYSTERY OF THE MIXED-UP ZOO
THE CAMP-OUT MYSTERY
THE MYSTERY GIRL
THE MYSTERY CRUISE

Contents

CHAPTER		PAGE
1.	Birthday Plans	1
2.	The Painting	12
3.	A Visit to Aunt Jane	26
4.	At the Museum	37
5.	Follow the Leader	47
6.	Another Strange Visit	56
7.	No More Clues?	67
8.	Surprise Visits	84
9.	Happy Endings	108

CHAPTER 1

Birthday Plans

The Alden children, Henry, Jessie, Violet, and Benny, ran out of their grandfather's house, laughing. They raced each other to the nearby garden with a fountain in the middle near where their boxcar stood.

Henry, who was fourteen and the oldest, reached the boxcar first and pulled open the door. Jessie and Violet got there next, at the same time. They turned and watched six-year-old Benny, puffing in the hot August sun, catch up with them.

"It's not fair," Benny said. "I'm always going to be the youngest and *never* win a race with you."

"Someday you'll beat even Henry," Violet said reassuringly. Though she was only ten she often seemed more considerate than many older people.

The children climbed into the boxcar, followed by their dog, Watch, and looked around.

"Whew," Benny said, "it's so dirty."

Henry got the broom Jessie had made when they had all lived in the boxcar, and started sweeping the floor. "We haven't been in here for a while. That's why it's so dusty. But I like it anyway."

Jessie smiled and spoke in the voice she used when she wanted to sound older than twelve. "Remember when we ran away and lived here after mother and father died? I think I can remember every day. Remember how we hid from Grandfather?"

"Yes," Benny said, "because we thought

he was mean and we wouldn't like living with him."

"And look how wonderful and kind he is," Violet said. "And how happy we are with him."

"That's why we're here," Henry said. "Because we love him and want to plan a wonderful party for his birthday next month. We have a lot of work to do."

"Let's get started then," Jessie said. "It's awfully hot in here."

"Wait," Benny interrupted. "First let's eat. I'm — "

"Hungry," Violet finished for him. She reached for the basket she had brought with her. "Mrs. McGregor packed a little snack for us."

Jessie went to the shelf that held the dishes they had found and used when they lived in the boxcar. She took four cups.

But Violet said, "We only need three. I brought Benny's cup from the house. I couldn't forget Benny's cup."

Benny took a cracked pink cup from the basket and held it out. Henry lifted out spice cookies and a carton of milk and filled Benny's cup. Jessie took peaches and plums and put them in a bowl. Then she piled bananas on top of the fresh fruit.

The boxcar was exactly the same as it had been when the children had lived in it, except that Mrs. McGregor had given the children four plump, brightly colored cushions so they could sit on them on the floor. Now they got comfortable and chewed on the delicious cookies.

"Well," Jessie asked, "what should we do for Grandfather's party?"

"We have to have a cake and ice cream," Benny said positively. "You can't have a birthday party without a cake."

"I'll help Mrs. McGregor bake the cake," Jessie said.

"No! I'll do that," Benny shouted.

Violet laughed. "I knew you'd say that. Well, I'll play the violin for Grandfather. I'll

be glad to do *that.* I'll have to think about what to play."

"And I'll decorate the dining room," Jessie said.

"I think I'll write a poem," Henry said. "We were studying poetry in school at the end of the term. I'll be able to put what I learned to good use."

"We have to buy him a present, too," Violet said. "What should it be?"

"Model cars," Benny said.

The other children laughed. Henry said, "I saw Grandfather looking at a sweater in Barlow's Men's Shop last week. I think he liked it. We could all chip in, and I'll buy it."

"I don't have much money," Benny said, thoughtfully. "I won't be able to pay my share."

"We'll work all that out, Benny. Don't worry," Jessie said, patting his shoulder.

Violet suddenly jumped up. "I know. Let's dress up for the party."

"You mean I have to wear a tie?" Benny asked mournfully.

"No," Violet said. "I mean dress up in costume. There are all kinds of old clothes in the attic. We could use those. It will be like a masquerade. Grandfather would love it. I know it."

"That's a wonderful idea," Jessie said eagerly.

Henry made a face. "I don't know. Dressing up is sort of childish. Don't you think?"

"No!" Violet and Jessie said at the same time.

"Come on," Jessie grabbed Henry's hand. "Let's go up to the attic right now. I know you'll like dressing up."

They ran back to the house and into the front hall. Watch raced in after them. Mrs. McGregor came out of the kitchen with flour on her hands and nose. "What's all the excitement about? Where are you all off to in such a hurry?"

"We're going up to the attic so we can find

dress up clothes for Grandfather's party," Violet said, catching her breath.

"What party? What's this all about?" Mrs. McGregor asked.

"We'll tell you later," Jessie shouted as they all ran for the stairs.

"Open the windows up there. It must be a hundred degrees in that attic," Mrs. McGregor called after them.

Upstairs, Jessie pulled open a window. "Whew! Mrs. McGregor was right. It's *really* hot in here."

Violet was already poking around. She found an old, big straw hat and tried it on. She ran to a standing mirror and giggled at her image.

"It's just right for you," Jessie cried. "It's lavender. Your favorite color."

Henry found a velvet coat and slipped into it. "How about this?"

Benny had opened a trunk and was pulling out old toys — blocks and balls and a jump rope and a jack-in-the-box. "I like it up here. I'm glad we came."

Jessie was now standing silently in a corner with her back to her brothers and sister. Violet looked at her. "What did you find, Jessie?"

Slowly, Jessie turned around. In her hands she had a small painting in a carved gold frame. "Look, how beautiful this is," she said.

Violet put down the hat and moved toward Jessie. "Ooh, you're right, she is beautiful," she gasped. "I don't think I'd ever get tired of looking at it."

The painting was of a lovely young woman in an evening gown. Around her throat was a necklace of sparkling blue sapphires that matched her eyes. The woman was staring out of the picture with wide eyes, and she had a small smile on her red lips. She looked very happy.

"Who do you suppose she is?" Benny asked.

Henry moved closer to the painting. "She looks like the pictures Grandfather has shown us of Grandmother."

"But those pictures were of an older lady," Jessie said.

"Well," Violet said thoughtfully, "this could have been painted when Grandmother was much younger."

"But if this is Grandmother, why is the picture hidden away up here?" Henry wondered.

Benny shrugged. "Why don't we ask Grandfather. He'll know. Grandfather always knows everything."

Jessie laughed. "Benny, you always get right to the point."

CHAPTER 2

The Painting

After dinner, when the whole family was settled in the big living room, Jessie ran up to her room and brought down the portrait. She took it over to her grandfather and held it out to him.

"Grandfather," she said softly. "We found this in the attic today. We're all wondering who this lovely lady is. Henry thinks it's Grandmother, but this lady looks so young."

Mr. Alden stared at the picture. He seemed to have drifted off into another world. Looking at her grandfather's sad face, Violet said immediately, "It doesn't matter,

Grandfather. We'll take the picture right back to the attic."

She picked up the painting, but Mr. Alden held out a hand to her. "It's all right, Violet. You can leave it here."

"Is this our grandmother?" she asked.

Grandfather smiled. "Yes, it is. It was painted when she was a very young woman, and very beautiful. But then, she was beautiful until the day she died."

"Why was it up in the attic?" Benny asked. "Why isn't it hanging right here?" Benny pointed to the wall over the fireplace.

Grandfather sighed. "Well, children, it's a long story. All of you sit down and I'll tell you."

Benny and Violet sat at Mr. Alden's feet. Jessie and Henry sat on the sofa next to Grandfather's easy chair. They all looked at him, waiting for him to go on.

Grandfather cleared his throat. "I gave your grandmother — her name was Celia — the necklace she is wearing in the portrait as a wedding present. I had had it designed by a very talented jeweler. It was one of a kind. There was no other just like it anywhere. Your grandmother loved it so much she had this portrait painted of her wearing her precious wedding present. A year after our wedding, we had a big party to celebrate our first anniversary and, of course, she wore the necklace.

"Oh, it was a wonderful party, with food made by the best caterer in town and an orchestra and beautiful flowers. When the party was over, Celia put the necklace in its velvet box and placed the box in her dressing table drawer. She intended to put it in the safe the next day."

"What happened then?" Benny asked breathlessly.

"Well," Mr. Alden continued, "she was so busy the next day helping the caterers gather together all the dishes and glasses and pots they had brought to the house that she forgot about the necklace. Until that night. She opened her drawer and took out the velvet

jewelry box . . . but it was empty. The necklace was gone."

"Oh, no!" Jessie cried out.

"Where was it?" Benny asked, his eyes
wide with surprise.

Grandfather shrugged. "We never found
it. We looked all over. The police came the
next day and questioned everyone who had
been in the house the day before. Everyone — all the people who worked for the caterer, every delivery person, everyone. They
even questioned me! But no one knew anything or had seen anything. The necklace was
gone forever."

"But the picture," Violet asked softly,
"why is it in the attic?"

Grandfather sighed again. "I had hung the
painting right over the mantelpiece after it
was painted. I loved looking at it. But once
the necklace disappeared, your grandmother
couldn't bear to look at the painting. It always reminded her of the wedding present
she had so loved that was gone. So we took

the painting down and put it up in the attic. After all these years, I had forgotten it was still there."

"That is such a sad story, Grandfather," Jessie said.

Grandfather smiled. The sadness was gone from his face. "Well, Jessie, that was a long time ago. But I will tell you, that as the oldest granddaughter the necklace would have been yours."

"Oh, Jessie, look what you might have had," Benny said.

The children laughed and Grandfather stood up. "Why don't we all go into the kitchen and see if there is any of Mrs. McGregor's chocolate cake left."

"And some milk," Benny added.

Grandfather laughed and put his arm around Benny's shoulders. "And some milk," he agreed.

They all sat around the big table in the cheerful kitchen. Grandfather poured milk for each of them and Jessie cut slices of cake.

"That's the end of *this* chocolate cake," she said, rinsing the empty plate under hot water.

"Maybe Mrs. McGregor will make another one tomorrow," Benny said hopefully.

"Or a lemon meringue pie," Henry said, just as hopefully.

As they ate their snack, Jessie said, "Grandfather, it's so sad that Grandmother's necklace just disappeared. Grandmother looked so lovely wearing it, too."

Grandfather smiled. "Yes, she did. I'm glad that she had it to enjoy for a little while anyway."

"Are you *sure* the police really talked to everyone who might have known *anything* about it?" Henry asked.

"Absolutely," Mr. Alden said. "I was surprised at how many people they thought of to question. It was embarrassing, because they insisted on talking to all of our guests, too. And some of them weren't very happy about that. They felt it was insulting. But the detective in charge of the case insisted."

Mr. Alden smiled. "You can't imagine where they looked for the necklace, too. As upset as we were at the time, your grandmother and I laughed."

"Where?" Violet asked with interest.

"Would you believe even in the refrigerator?"

The children laughed. "Why the refrigerator?" Jessie asked.

"Well," Mr. Alden said, "they said it wasn't impossible that the thief might have put it there just for a little while . . . until he or she could get it out of the house."

"That seems sort of silly," Henry said.

"It did to me, too," Mr. Alden said. "And it wasn't in the refrigerator, anyway. But it did make a good story for a couple of years. It did make your grandmother laugh."

"Grandfather," Jessie said thoughtfully, "you said that Grandmother opened the jewelry box and it was empty."

"That's right, Jessie," Mr. Alden said.

"What did you do with the box?" Jessie

asked. "It must have always reminded Grandmother of the theft."

"You're right," Grandfather said. "So I took the empty box and put it in a drawer in the desk in my den. That way your grandmother wouldn't keep seeing it."

"And then did you throw it away?" Benny asked.

"No, children, believe it or not, I still have that empty box," Mr. Alden said.

Violet's eyes widened. "Could we see it?" she asked.

"Of course," Mr. Alden said. "I still have it in the den."

They all walked into the little room that Grandfather had set up as an office at home. It was here that he did any work he brought home from his office. It was a comfortable room with a leather couch and an easy chair and a big desk. Mr. Alden opened a drawer in the mahogany desk and took out a square blue velvet box. He gently handed it to Violet.

Violet opened the box and looked at the

inside, which was lined with ivory-colored satin. There was a soft hollow that had once held the sapphire necklace. "I can almost *see* it," Violet said.

"Me too," Benny agreed.

"Well, now," Grandfather said cheerfully, "I don't want you children to be upset about this. So let's just forget about it. It's bedtime, anyway."

Later Jessie sat in Violet's bedroom and watched Violet brushing her hair. Anyone looking at the room would have immediately known it was Violet's. The wallpaper, the bedspread, and the curtains all had violets on them.

Violet stopped brushing and turned to Jessie. "What do you suppose happened to the necklace?"

"I don't know," Jessie answered, lying on her back on Violet's bed. "Grandfather said they questioned everybody and there were no clues at all."

Violet sighed. "What a shame. It looked like such a beautiful necklace. It would have been gorgeous around your neck, too."

They both laughed at the very idea of it and then forgot about the missing necklace when Watch came in and tried to jump up on the bed.

It rained for the next three days, and the Aldens were becoming more and more bored. One afternoon they were all in the boxcar. Henry was trying to write his poem for Grandfather's birthday. Violet and Benny were playing jacks, and Jessie was reading the Greenfield newspaper. Suddenly she let out a cry.

"Look," she shouted. She held out the paper with one hand and pointed to a picture with the other.

Henry, Violet, and Benny ran over and all stared at the paper. "Look at what?" Benny asked. "It's just a picture of a lady we don't know."

"Look at what she's wearing!" Jessie insisted.

Violet took the paper. "She's wearing an evening dress. It's very pretty. And the caption under the picture says: *Mrs. Elizabeth Harkins, who was the chairperson of the Elmford Hospital Dance.*"

"What *else* is she wearing?" Jessie asked impatiently.

Henry looked closer. "A necklace," he said.

"It looks *just* like the necklace in the painting," Jessie said.

Violet looked at the paper again. "Jessie, the necklace in this picture is so small and the picture is black and white. How can you tell anything from this?"

"I *know* they look alike," Jessie said. "Let's go back to the house and look at the painting again."

They all ran back and into the living room, where Grandfather had left the painting leaning against a bookcase. Jessie put the portrait down on the sofa and placed the newspaper picture right next to it. The children leaned over and looked at them both very closely.

"See!" Jessie said. "They *do* look alike!"

"I think she's right," Violet said.

Henry frowned. "I can't really tell."

Benny hopped on one foot with excitement. "Maybe we have another mystery. But how are we going to solve it? We don't even know that Mrs. Harkins."

Henry looked at the newspaper again. "Look! She lives in Elmford . . . where Aunt Jane lives. Maybe we could go to visit Aunt Jane and — "

"And talk to Mrs. Harkins," Jessie finished for him.

"We'll have to ask Grandfather if we can go," Violet said.

"He likes us to visit Aunt Jane," Benny assured her.

Henry looked thoughtful. "I don't think we should tell Grandfather about Mrs. Harkins. If it turns out her necklace is a different one from our grandmother's, he'd be so disappointed."

Violet agreed. "Henry is right. We don't want to upset Grandfather for no reason."

"All right," Jessie said. "We'll ask him about visiting Aunt Jane tonight."

Violet went over to the desk in a corner of the room and took a large sheet of white paper and a pencil out of a drawer.

"What are you doing?" Jessie asked.

Violet sat down next to the painting and, leaning on a large book, started to draw. "I'm going to copy the necklace very carefully. So, if we do get to talk to Mrs. Harkins, we can show her what *our* necklace looks like."

Benny watched her carefully. "But ours is blue."

Violet smiled. "Right. I'll color my picture when I'm finished."

"That's a great idea, Violet," Henry said, looking at his sister with admiration.

CHAPTER 3

A Visit to Aunt Jane

After dinner, all the Aldens sat out on the wide green lawn and enjoyed the soft, cool evening breeze. When the children told Mr. Alden they wanted to visit Aunt Jane, he agreed right away. He thought it was a fine idea.

"You haven't been away this summer at all," he said. "I'll call her right now."

Aunt Jane thought the visit was a fine idea, too. "I'll be especially happy to see you because Uncle Andy is away on business and I'm really lonesome," she told Jessie on the phone.

It was arranged that the Aldens would take the one o'clock bus the next day and Aunt Jane would be waiting at the bus stop for them.

In the morning they all packed small, brightly colored suitcases. Benny made sure his pink cup was in his. At one o'clock Grandfather drove them to the bus station and waved good-bye. At three they were in Elmford where Aunt Jane was waiting for them. They couldn't wait to get to Aunt Jane's old farmhouse, thinking of the cold water in the pond not far from her house, and how they'd enjoy splashing in it.

When they had unpacked and played in the creek for over an hour, they all joined Aunt Jane in her big kitchen. Benny tore lettuce for a dinner salad. Henry mashed potatoes. Violet cut string beans, and Jessie and Aunt Jane shaped turkey patties. Aunt Jane was very aware of healthy eating and tried to get the Aldens to enjoy her menus . . .

even the turkey patties instead of hamburg-
ers. They never told her they weren't crazy
about the turkey patties.

Violet and Jessie exchanged a glance.
Then Jessie quickly told Aunt Jane the story
of their finding the portrait and then seeing
Mrs. Harkins' picture in the newspaper.
Aunt Jane was astounded.

"Your grandmother's necklace has been
missing for years. I can't believe Mrs. Harkins' necklace is the same one," Aunt Jane
said, looking at the Aldens.

"Do you know Mrs. Harkins?" Henry
asked.

Aunt Jane shook her head. "A little. We
aren't really friends, but in a small town like
Elmford, everybody knows almost everybody else."

"Could you call her and ask if we could
talk to her?" Jessie asked, wiping her hands
on the apron she was wearing. She waited
eagerly for Aunt Jane's answer.

"I don't know," Aunt Jane replied. "I'm
not sure she'd want to be questioned by four

strange children she's never met."

"Try," Violet pleaded. "Please!"

"Please," Benny repeated.

"All right," Aunt Jane agreed. "I'll call her."

Aunt Jane went into the sitting room next to the kitchen and made her call. She came back and said, "Mrs. Harkins said you could come by at eleven tomorrow morning. She didn't seem too happy at the idea, but she did say she'd see you. She said to be on time."

Benny threw his arms around Aunt Jane. "You're a good aunt."

After breakfast the next morning, Aunt Jane told the Aldens exactly where Mrs. Harkins lived. They had all visited Aunt Jane so many times that they knew their way around town very well. They took the bikes Aunt Jane kept for them and rode through the green countryside, passing well-kept farms and small houses. The air smelled sweet and fresh.

"Look! Cows!" Benny shouted, pointing

to three cows grazing lazily behind a wire fence next to the road. "I like farms," he said positively.

"You just like cows, because they give you the milk you love so much," Jessie said, laughing.

The children pedaled slowly so that they arrived at Mrs. Harkins' just at eleven. They remembered her instructions to be on time. Her home was a large, redbrick house with white shuttered windows. A maid answered Jessie's ring and took them into a large, comfortable living room. Mrs. Harkins stood waiting for the Aldens.

She was a small, attractive woman of about fifty. "Well," she said. "Your aunt said you wanted to talk to me about a necklace . . . or something like that. Why would four young children be interested in a necklace?"

Jessie took the newspaper picture out of her pocket and showed it to Mrs. Harkins. "The necklace you're wearing — " she began.

"Why don't we all sit down," Elizabeth

Harkins said, leading them all into the living room. "We'll be more comfortable."

"The necklace — " Jessie continued.

"It looks like our grandmother's," Benny blurted out.

Mrs. Harkins frowned. "I don't understand."

Violet reached into her knapsack and smoothed out her drawing of the Alden necklace. "You see, our grandmother had this necklace. We think it looks like the one you wore to the dance."

Suddenly a man appeared in the doorway. "Elizabeth," he said firmly, "please come in here."

Mrs. Harkins stood up. "Excuse me. My husband wants to talk to me."

She walked into the next room. First there was just a murmur of voices. Then the sounds were louder, as if the Harkins were arguing. The Aldens looked at each other.

"Maybe we should leave," Violet said. "I think we've upset them."

Mr. Harkins then said, loud enough to be

heard in the next room, "Be careful!"

Mrs. Harkins came back and sat down again. "I really only have a couple of minutes to talk to you children. What do you want?" Her voice was cold.

Henry said, "We just were wondering if your necklace could possibly be — "

Mrs. Harkins interrupted him. "The necklace isn't mine." Now she smiled. "The Elmford Museum lent it to me to wear to the dance, because it was a charity affair for the hospital. I don't know anything about the necklace at all."

She stood up and held her hand out to Jessie. "It was very nice meeting all of you. Now I have an appointment I must get to. I'll have to ask you to leave."

Outside the house, Benny said, "She wasn't very friendly. Was she?" He looked very puzzled.

Henry put an arm around Benny's shoulders. "You're right, Benny. She wasn't."

"What do we do now?" Violet asked.

"Eat!" Benny said. "I'm hungry."

Jessie turned to Henry. "Remember that nice little coffee shop on Main Street? Let's go there for lunch."

"Good idea," Benny said.

In minutes they were seated in a booth in the small coffee shop. "First let's order, then we can talk about Mrs. Harkins," Violet said.

When the waitress stopped at their table, Benny ordered a peanut-butter-and-jelly sandwich, chocolate cake, and milk. He smiled when he finished ordering.

"Can you eat that much, Benny?" Jessie asked.

"Sure can. Watch," Benny answered.

Henry ordered a grilled cheese and a cola. Jessie had tuna fish and a milk shake and Violet ordered a hamburger and milk. Then Jessie said, "I don't understand, if Mrs. Harkins doesn't even own the necklace, why was she so cold to us?"

"And why did Mr. Harkins tell her to 'Be careful'?" Henry asked.

"Well, I think the next thing to do is go

to the museum and talk to someone there," Jessie suggested.

"We'll do that right after lunch," Henry said.

As soon as they finished eating, the Alden children biked to the small museum. When they got there, they saw a sign on the door that read:

CLOSED ON MONDAY
HOURS: TUES–SUN. 12–5.

"Oh, no!" Violet cried out. "Maybe we should have called first."

"Now what should we do?" Benny asked. "I'm getting hot."

Henry glanced down the street where he saw a small movie theater. "How about a movie to escape the heat? It should be cool in there."

"Well," Benny said, thoughtfully, "if the movie's not mushy. I don't want to sit through a mushy movie."

Jessie laughed. "It isn't mushy at all. It's a western."

"Let's go!" Benny shouted.

"I'll call Aunt Jane and tell her we'll be home later," Violet said.

CHAPTER 4

At the Museum

The next day the Aldens were at the museum at exactly twelve o'clock. The entrance lobby was cool and quiet. The highly polished wood floors made their footsteps echo throughout the room. Henry pointed to an office to their right. They all walked to the door and peered in.

"Anyone here?" Henry called out.

A small, gray-haired man came out of a supply closet. In his hands were some pads of paper. He smoothed his mustache and walked toward the Aldens.

"Can I help you?" he asked, smiling. "I'm Carl Mason."

At first the children were silent, not knowing where to begin. Then Jessie said, "Mrs. Harkins told us the necklace she wore to the hospital dance belonged to the museum."

"Indeed it does," Mr. Mason said. "But why are you youngsters interested in the necklace?"

"Because we think it belonged to our grandmother," Benny blurted out.

Mr. Mason laughed loudly. "That's a good joke!"

"Could we see your necklace?" Violet asked.

"No reason not," Mr. Mason replied. "Follow me." He led the children to a small room with a display case in the center. In the case was the necklace. It glittered under the light.

"Oh," Violet whispered. "It's so beautiful."

"Oh, yes," Jessie agreed. She took the newspaper picture and Violet's drawing out

of her pocket and put them on top of the display case.

The Aldens gathered closer and looked at the necklace and the pictures.

Quickly Henry explained about the necklace to Mr. Mason.

"So you think this necklace might be your grandmother's?" Mr. Mason asked.

Jessie examined Violet's drawing again. "It looks like your necklace. Don't you think so?"

Mr. Mason laughed again. "First of all, there are probably many necklaces that look exactly like these."

"Oh, no," Violet said. "Grandfather said his was designed just for our grandmother."

"Well now, children," Mr. Mason said, "you know that everyone isn't always totally honest. This designer might not have kept his word."

Benny looked upset. "Oh!" he said.

Mr. Mason looked at the Aldens and cleared his throat. "Why don't you just leave this drawing? When I have more time, I'll look at it closely."

Violet frowned. "When do you think that will be?"

"I don't know," Mr. Mason said, curtly. "Come back tomorrow afternoon after three. We'll talk again *if* I have time." Mr. Mason led the Aldens to the front door and made sure they left.

As they walked to their bikes, Benny said, "I don't think anyone in this town likes us."

Violet laughed and put an arm around him. "*I* like you," she said.

Jessie sighed and said, "Let's go back to the pond and cool off."

"Right," Henry agreed. "First, we can to to that little market." He pointed to a store across the street. "We'll buy things for lunch and take Aunt Jane on a picnic."

"You're a smart brother," Benny said, heading for the store.

In the market, they bought bread and ham and cheese for sandwiches. Benny lifted a container of chocolate milk from a case. Violet picked out fresh fruit while Jessie added cookies to their order.

Aunt Jane was folding laundry in the kitchen when the children came home. "We're going to take you out to lunch," Benny told Aunt Jane proudly.

"Right," Henry said. "We're going to picnic at the pond."

"Wonderful," Aunt Jane said. And then she asked, "What happened at the museum?"

She listened with total attention as the Aldens took turns telling her about their conversation with Mr. Mason.

"We did see the necklace," Violet said. "It's *so* beautiful."

"I think it could be Grandmother's," Jessie said.

As the children made the sandwiches and packed the picnic basket, Aunt Jane thought about their visit to the museum. Finally she said, "It is really very hard to believe that after all these years, the necklace in the museum is the Alden necklace."

"I think Aunt Jane is probably right," Henry said. "After all when the robbery took place it must have been reported in the Greenfield newspaper. Elmford isn't *that* far away. People here would have read about it."

Aunt Jane thought for a moment. "As a matter of fact, it wasn't in the Greenfield paper. The printing press was broken and the paper wasn't published for a week. I remember your grandfather telling me that."

"I'm tired of the necklace," Benny said. "Let's go to the pond."

At the pond, Uncle Andy had hung a big, old rubber tire to a tree on a long rope. One by one the Aldens sat in the center of the tire, swung out over the pond, and dropped in. Benny and Henry went in together, since the middle of the pond was over Benny's head. They all forgot about the necklace as they sailed out over the pond and then fell in.

They didn't think about it much either, while they ate dinner and listened to Aunt Jane tell funny stories about her growing-up years. When the phone rang in the next room, Aunt Jane said, "Jessie dear, will you answer it?"

Jessie ran in and picked up the receiver. "Hello," she said.

A woman's voice asked, "Who is this?"

Jessie said, "I'm Jessie Alden . . . Jane Bean's niece. I'm visiting her for a few days."

"I think you should go home," the woman said. "I think you and your brothers should just go home. Right away."

"Who is this?" Jessie asked nervously.

But all she heard was the phone being hung up.

Slowly Jessie walked back into the kitchen.

"Who was it?" Aunt Jane asked.

"It was a woman who said we should all go home . . . right away. When I asked who it was, she just hung up."

Henry said angrily, "Well, she had some nerve."

"Did you recognize the voice?" Violet asked.

"Was it that Mrs. Harkins, who didn't like us?" Benny asked.

"It didn't sound like her at all. But I don't know *who* it was," Jessie replied.

"I don't like this," Aunt Jane said. "Not one bit. Maybe you *should* go home. Maybe I should call your grandfather and tell him — "

"Oh, no," Jessie interrupted. "We want to try to find out about the necklace just a little bit longer. Think how happy Grandfather would be if we found the necklace."

"He'd love that," Aunt Jane said, "but he wouldn't want any harm to come to you children. He'd be very angry with me if I let that happen."

"Aunt Jane," Henry said, "we're not going to get hurt. It's probably just someone playing a joke on us."

"Except," Benny said, "we don't know anyone here who would *play* a joke on us."

They all silently agreed with Benny.

"We have to go back to the museum tomorrow," Violet said.

"Please," Jessie added.

"Well, all right," Aunt Jane finally said. "But I'm going with you. I'll drive you into town and we'll *all* talk to Mr. Mason together."

CHAPTER 5

Follow the Leader

The Aldens could hardly wait until it was time to go to the museum. They ate breakfast and lunch as slowly as they could so the time would pass. They played three games of badminton. Finally, they all piled into Aunt Jane's car and drove into town.

When they got to the museum, Mr. Mason looked startled to see Aunt Jane. Violet and Jessie exchanged a glance when they saw Mr. Mason's surprised face. "Well, Mrs. Bean," he said, "I didn't expect to see *you* here."

"I just thought I'd drive the Aldens into town," she said.

"Mr. Mason," Henry asked, "have you had time to look at Violet's drawing of the necklace yet?"

"Well now, young man," Carl Mason began. "A very strange thing happened. The drawing is gone."

"Gone!" Violet and Jessie said at the same time.

Mr. Mason cleared his throat. "The cleaning man was here last night, and I guess in his effort to straighten up my desk he just threw out some things he shouldn't have. I'm really very sorry."

All the Aldens secretly thought he didn't *look* sorry.

"My sister took a lot of time to make that drawing," Benny said. "I'll bet she feels really bad that you threw out her picture. It was very good, too."

Violet raised her chin and looked at Mr. Mason. "It's all right, Benny. I can make another one when I get home."

"Well, my dear, you just do that," Mr. Mason said.

Aunt Jane took Benny by the hand and said, "Mr. Mason, I wonder if I could see the necklace, please."

Carl Mason looked very unhappy. "Of course, Mrs. Bean. Just come right this way."

They all walked into the room that held the display case. Aunt Jane looked at the necklace and said softly, "It *is* lovely."

Suddenly, Jessie said, "Look! I didn't notice this yesterday." She pointed to a small card on the lower part of the case. She read out loud, "Donated by Mrs. Lorraine Newton."

"What does that word *donated* mean?" Benny asked.

"It means that the necklace was given as a gift to the museum by Mrs. Newton," Henry said.

"Who is *she*?" Benny asked.

"Mrs. Lorraine Newton is a very important person in Elmford," Mr. Mason said.

"She is a very wealthy and well-known woman here."

"And the necklace is hers?" Violet asked.

"Well, it *was* hers, until she very generously gave it to the museum. That was many years ago," Mr. Mason said. "Really, that's all I can tell you."

Aunt Jane said, "I'm sorry to have bothered you, Mr. Mason. I guess it's time we left." She guided the children out of the museum.

In the car driving home, Aunt Jane said, "I know what you are all thinking. You want to visit Mrs. Newton, but I don't think you can do that. The necklace *must* have been hers. You can't just go and ask her a lot of questions."

"Not a lot," Henry said. "Just a few."

"I don't know," Aunt Jane said.

"We can't go home without talking to Mrs. Newton," Jessie said. "We just can't."

"I doubt that she'll even see you," Aunt Jane said.

"Can't we try?" Jessie asked.

Aunt Jane laughed. "Well, I do admit you are the most determined children I've ever known. You get it from your grandfather. All right, but don't bother the poor woman longer than a few minutes."

Aunt Jane looked at Henry who was sitting next to her. The other children were in the backseat. "Henry, you keep looking at the side mirror. Is there something bothering you?"

Henry didn't take his eyes off the mirror. "Aunt Jane, someone is following us."

Jessie, Benny, and Violet immediately turned around and looked out of the back window. Benny was now kneeling on the seat.

"Henry, what an imagination you have," Aunt Jane said. "Why would anyone want to follow us?"

"I think it's Mr. Mason," Jessie said, staring out of the window.

"Oh, Jessie," Aunt Jane said, laughing. "You've been playing detective too many

times. Mr. Mason would have no reason to follow us."

"Aunt Jane," Henry said, "just to test him, make a right turn at the corner."

Aunt Jane turned the car, and the car behind turned right, too.

"See," Benny said, "he turned, too. He *is* following us."

Aunt Jane laughed. "Well, maybe the man wanted to go right because he lives near here. I'm going back to the main road and I'm going to take you all to Kenniston Park. It's wonderful there. We'll rent a boat and go rowing, and we'll eat there, too. Maybe it will take your minds off the necklace. I hope it will."

But the children all kept looking at the car behind them. When they left Elmford and were riding toward Kenniston, the car behind them disappeared.

"See," Aunt Jane said cheerfully. "It's gone."

"Yes," Henry agreed. "But it only turned off when we left Elmford."

*   *   *

When they got to Kenniston Park, they went to the lake, where Aunt Jane rented the largest rowboat. The Aldens sat two by two opposite each other, and Aunt Jane sat in the back. Violet and Jessie rowed together and then Benny and Henry. Aunt Jane trailed her hand in the cool water and watched the Aldens pulling on the oars. All of them loved every minute and they were all able to forget about the necklace.

Then they walked to a food stand in the park and bought hot dogs and bags of potato chips and sodas. They sat on the grass by the lake while they ate.

"Mrs. McGregor wouldn't approve of us eating this kind of dinner," Violet said, smiling.

"Well," Aunt Jane said, "I don't like eating junk food either, but it can't hurt once in a while."

They finished their food and sat quietly watching the sky darken, and lights come on in the park. Music came from somewhere in the distance. Benny fell asleep with his head in Jessie's lap. When it was time to leave, Henry carried him to the car. The Aldens all agreed it had been a wonderful night. But every now and then, Jessie and Violet and Henry each thought of the sparkling sapphire necklace in the display case in the now dark museum.

CHAPTER 6

Another Strange Visit

The next morning Aunt Jane was out in the garden cutting flowers while the Aldens ate breakfast. "We have to see Mrs. Newton this morning," Jessie said. "Soon Grandfather will want us to come home. I know he misses us."

Violet said, "We'll have to call her first."

"I don't know," Henry said, thoughtfully. "Maybe we should just go without calling her."

Violet shook her head. "It isn't polite to do that," she said.

"Well, it isn't polite for her to have our

grandmother's necklace, either," Benny said firmly.

Jessie and Henry laughed and even Violet had to smile. "You know, Benny's right," Henry said.

They finished their breakfast of cold cereal, buttered toast with jam, and milk, and went upstairs to dress. "We all have to look spic-and-span," Jessie said. "So we can impress Mrs. Newton with what nice children we are."

Jessie and Violet both put on flowered skirts and blouses. Jessie's was sparkling white and Violet's lavender. Benny and Henry wore khaki pants and white shirts. When they came downstairs, Aunt Jane was arranging her flowers.

"I can guess where you're going," she said. "But did you call Mrs. Newton?"

Jessie and Henry exchanged a guilty look. "We thought we'd just go. Just for a few minutes," he added quickly. "We won't stay long."

Aunt Jane smiled. "I know I shouldn't

agree, but just promise you won't stay long."

"Absolutely," Jessie said.

"Positively," Benny added.

The Aldens followed the directions Aunt Jane gave them to Mrs. Newton's house. They gasped when they arrived. The house was three stories high with big columns at the front and a circular driveway leading up to it. There were beautiful rosebushes on either side. The Aldens rode up, left their bikes in the grass, and rang the doorbell. A woman opened the door and looked at the Aldens. Her face was unsmiling. She was silent for a moment.

"Yes?" she finally said.

Jessie looked at her sister and brothers and then said, "I'm Jessie Alden. These are my brothers and my sister. We wondered if we could talk to Mrs. Lorraine Newton. Are you her?"

"No," the woman answered. "I'm her daughter, Laura Newton Garrison. My mother is out on the back patio. Follow me. We've been expecting you."

Inside the house, Violet asked, "You've been expecting us?"

"Yes," Laura Garrison said. "Mr. Mason called yesterday and said that you had been at the museum, asking a lot of questions. He was sure you would pay us a visit."

Mrs. Garrison led the Aldens through a large living room out onto a sunny patio. A white-haired woman in a flowered summer dress was sitting stiffly in a green wicker chair. She looked at the Alden children coldly.

"Tell me what you want," she ordered.

Once again, the Aldens told the tale of the necklace. "I don't have the drawing I made," Violet said. "Mr. Mason said someone must have thrown it away. So you can't see just what we mean. But . . ."

Benny looked at Mrs. Newton and said, "Our grandfather would be *so* happy if we could find his necklace and give it — "

Laura Garrison interrupted Benny and looked at her mother. "Mother, maybe we should — " There was a sad tone to her voice.

"Laura!" Mrs. Newton said, as if she were warning her daughter.

"You children have been imagining this whole necklace story. It is definitely *not* your grandmother's. I *know* it. The necklace has been in my family for generations. It has been handed down from one generation to another."

"What's a generation?" Benny whispered to Henry.

"I'll tell you later," Henry replied.

Laura looked at her mother again. "Mother, I think it is time — "

"I think it is time," Mrs. Newton said, "for these children to have some juice and then go home." She remained unsmiling. She leaned forward and poured a glass of grape juice from a pitcher on the table in front of her. She handed a glass to each of the Aldens. When she reached over to give Jessie hers, it

slipped from her hand and crashed to the ground. Drops of the purple juice splattered all over Jessie's white blouse.

"Oh," Jessie cried out. She stood up and wiped at her blouse. Somehow, she felt this had not been an accident.

Mrs. Newton handed Jessie a napkin and said, "I think you should go home and wash your shirt immediately. That will get the stains out."

"But the necklace," Violet said. "What about . . ."

Mrs. Newton stood up. "My dear child, the necklace was *mine*. *I* gave it to the museum. That's the end of the story. You must simply give up your silly ideas. We have talked about this enough."

The children all stood. "Thank you for seeing us," Henry said.

Mrs. Newton nodded. "I hope you will all go back to Greenfield now and forget about this."

Laura led the Aldens to the front hall. "I know my mother can be rather cold sometimes. She doesn't mean to be. She really doesn't."

Jessie stopped at a mirror over a table in the hall and looked in to see how stained her shirt was. She glanced down at the table and saw an unopened envelope. It was addressed to Mrs. Lorraine Newton, but the return address was a Mrs. Susan Barstow at 1600 Hudson Lane in Silver City. Silver City was the town next to Greenfield.

Jessie didn't say anything to the other Aldens about the letter she'd seen. She wanted to think about it first. When they reached Aunt Jane's they told her about Mrs. Newton.

"Well," Aunt Jane said, "I guess that is that. The necklace must belong to Mrs. Newton."

Violet nodded. "I guess you're right. I think we should call Grandfather and tell him we are coming home tomorrow. I miss him a lot."

Aunt Jane agreed. "I'll be sorry to see you

all go, but I think Violet is right. You should go home."

Henry frowned. "I hate to go like this. I guess this will just have to be one mystery we aren't going to solve. It sure is a disappointment!"

Jessie called Mr. Alden. When she hung up she was smiling. "He sounded so happy that we were coming home. He said he'd tell Watch to expect us, too."

The next day they all kissed Aunt Jane good-bye. "Call me and let me know you got home safely," she said to them at the bus stop.

"We will," Benny promised.

At home Grandfather welcomed them. He had left his mill early so that he could meet his grandchildren at the Greenfield bus stop. He drove them to the house and they all sat outside in the late afternoon sun, drinking lemonade. Watch ran from one child to the other, nuzzling their hands, happy to have his family around.

"Tell me what you did at Aunt Jane's," Grandfather said.

The children exchanged a quick look.

"Well," Benny said, "we swung in an old tire at the pond."

"We went to Kenniston Park," Violet carefully said.

"And we went to the museum," Jessie added.

"Twice," Benny said.

Mr. Alden looked impressed. "I think that's fine, having that much of an interest in the Elmford Museum."

"It certainly *was* interesting," Benny said, smiling.

When Mrs. McGregor called them in for dinner, Mr. Alden said, "I want you to stop in the living room first and see something."

When they reached the door of the room, Violet gasped. "Look!"

Over the mantelpiece was their grandmother's portrait. "I thought it was time to put it up again," Mr. Alden said. "Even though I don't have the necklace, I do have the picture. We should enjoy it."

"I wish we had the necklace, too," Benny said.

"So do I," Grandfather said in agreement. "So do I."

CHAPTER 7

No More Clues?

The next afternoon the children were in the boxcar, playing Monopoly. Suddenly Jessie put the dice down. "I have something to tell you," she said.

"What?" Benny shouted. "It sounds like another mystery."

"It's the same mystery," Jessie said. "Do you remember when we were leaving Mrs. Newton's, I stopped to look in the mirror?"

"I remember," Violet answered.

"Well," Jessie continued. "There was a letter on the table under the mirror. It was addressed to Mrs. Newton, but the return address was a Mrs. Susan Barstow in Silver City."

"That's right near here," Henry said. "But I don't see what's so strange about that. What are you thinking?"

Jessie shrugged. "I don't know. It just seemed funny to me. Mrs. Newton getting a letter from a place so near here."

"I don't follow you, Jessie," Henry said. "What do you want to do?"

"I thought, maybe, we could just bike ride over there and well . . ."

"Do what?" Violet asked.

"Just look at the house, I guess," Jessie answered.

"What are you looking *for*?" Benny asked.

"I just can't believe we are at a dead end," Jessie said. "Maybe we'll see something at Mrs. Barstow's. I don't know what. But it can't hurt to look."

"I guess it can't hurt," Violet agreed.

"Let's go!" Benny said.

They ran up to the house and into the

kitchen where Mrs. McGregor was making spaghetti sauce. "We're going for a bike ride," Jessie said.

Mrs. McGregor looked away from the pot she was stirring. "Be careful and don't be late for dinner."

"We won't," Henry said.

"Was that a lie?" Benny asked, as they all took their bikes from the garage.

"No, it wasn't, Benny. We *are* going for a bike ride," Henry said.

"We just didn't say *where* we're going," Violet said.

"And Mrs. McGregor didn't ask, so that's okay," Henry added.

"Okay," Benny said.

They rode along, enjoying the warm sun and the fresh smells of summer grass. When they got to Silver City they stopped and asked a policeman the way to 1600 Hudson Lane. It was small and white with blue shutters and a neat little garden in front. The Aldens stopped behind a hedge to the left of the house and got off their bikes.

"Now that we're here," Henry said, "what are we looking for?"

Jessie said, "I guess I really don't know. I just didn't want to give up."

They waited for five minutes, but no one came out of the house. "I'm bored," Benny said.

Violet laughed. "At least you're not hungry."

"I'm hungry, too," Benny said, smiling mischievously.

Just then a car pulled up. "Look!" Jessie whispered.

Laura Garrison walked up the path to the house and rang the bell. The door opened and she went inside.

"I wonder what she's doing here?" Violet said.

"Well, if Mrs. Barstow writes to Mrs. Newton, Laura might know her, too. So it's not so strange if she visits Mrs. Barstow," Henry said.

They waited silently, watching the house.

Finally, Laura Garrison came out. The Aldens couldn't see who was in the doorway, but a woman's voice was loud enough for them to hear. "I will never agree to what you want, Laura. Never!"

"I think you're wrong, Susan — you and my mother," Laura replied.

Then she went back to her car and drove away.

"What do you suppose *that* meant?" Jessie said, thoughtfully.

"I don't think we'll ever know," Henry answered. "Let's go home."

"Maybe we should talk to Mrs. Barstow?" Jessie said.

"Jessie, what would you say to her?" Violet asked.

"I don't know. I just hate to go without talking to her," Jessie said.

Henry frowned slightly. "Chances are Mrs. Garrison is just a friend of this Mrs. Barstow. Nothing more than that. Let's not jump to conclusions."

Jessie shook her head, disagreeing. "Then

why did she shout at Mrs. Garrison and say, 'I will never agree to what you want'?"

"That didn't sound very friendly to me," Benny said.

The Aldens stood in silence for a few minutes. Then Henry said, "Well if we did go in, what would you ask her?"

"I'd just ask if she knew anything about the necklace," Jessie answered.

"How can we just go up and ring her bell? We don't even know her," Violet said. "That's very rude."

"We went to Mrs. Newton without calling," Benny reminded them.

"Right," Violet said, "and I thought that wasn't polite, either."

Jessie looked so downcast that Violet touched her arm and said, "All right, Jessie, we'll do it."

A smile lit up Jessie's face. "You don't have to worry. I'll do all the talking."

The children went up the walk to Mrs. Barstow's house and rang the bell. Soon a tall, thin woman with dark brown hair opened the door. She smiled and said, "I'm sorry but I've bought all the cookies I can manage to eat in the next year."

Benny looked at her in awe. "You *have?*"

"Excuse me, Mrs. Barstow, but we aren't selling anything. I wondered if we could talk to you for just a few minutes?" Jessie asked politely.

Susan Barstow looked surprised. "About what?" she asked.

"About our grandmother's necklace," Benny said quickly.

The smile left Susan Barstow's face. "What necklace?" she asked.

Violet asked shyly, "Couldn't we come in for just a little while?"

Mrs. Barstow thought for a minute and then said, "Just for a few minutes. But I can tell you right away that I don't know anything about any necklace."

She led them into a small living room and beckoned to them to sit down. Jessie, in as few words as possible, told the story again of the Alden necklace and their visits to Mrs. Harkins and Mrs. Newton.

Susan Barstow didn't meet the children's eyes. She looked out of the window and carefully said, "I can't help you at all. I've never heard of the necklace you're talking about."

Suddenly a whistling sound came from the kitchen. "My teakettle is boiling," Mrs. Barstow said. "I'll be right back."

When Mrs. Barstow was out of the room, Jessie looked around. Suddenly she jumped up and walked over to the mantelpiece. "Look," she cried.

The other children ran over to her. Jessie pointed to a large framed picture on the mantel. It was of Mrs. Newton and two small boys. It was an old picture, but Mrs. Newton was easily recognizable.

"It's that Mrs. Newton," Benny said.

"Yes," Jessie replied. "*See.*"

The teakettle stopped whistling and Henry whispered, "Jessie, what does that picture prove?"

"Well," Jessie answered, "they do know each other."

"We guessed that before," Violet whispered.

Mrs. Barstow came back into the room. It seemed to the Alden children that she paled a little when she saw them looking at the picture. "I don't have much time," she said.

Jessied pointed to the photograph. "Isn't that Mrs. Newton?"

Susan Barstow nodded. "Yes, it is. She's a very good friend of mine, and has been for years. That's a picture of her with my children, taken a number of years ago."

"Oh," Jessie said. She didn't know anything else to say or ask.

Mrs. Barstow's face softened a little. "You children should just go home and forget about the necklace nonsense. If someone stole your grandfather's necklace, I can't give you any help. I don't know anything about it."

Jessie said softly, "That was Laura Garrison who was here. We saw her before we came in."

The softness left Mrs. Barstow's face. "Laura is a friend of mine also. Now I have to ask you all to leave, and I also must ask you not to bother me or Mrs. Newton anymore."

"We're sorry if we bothered you," Violet said apologetically. "We won't do it again."

The children left and started biking home. "I think she's hiding *something*," Jessie said.

"Jessie," Henry replied, "everything she said could be true: Mrs. Newton is her friend. If Mrs. Newton is her friend, she would certainly know Laura Garrison. Maybe we *are* imagining things."

"I believe Jessie," Benny said loyally.

"I don't know," Violet said. "I think maybe Jessie is right. But there's nothing else we can do anyway."

After dinner that night, Mr. Alden took his grandchildren to town to a big ice cream parlor. They all ordered double cones and, as they were leaving, Laura Garrison came in with a man. When she saw the Aldens she smiled slightly. "This is my husband. We had dinner in Greenfield tonight," she said. She turned to her husband. "These are the Alden children I told you about."

Mr. Garrison looked at his wife. "Maybe we should all sit down and talk."

Mrs. Garrison stared at him for a moment and her cheeks got paler. "I don't think so. Mother wouldn't . . ."

She stopped talking, took her husband's arm, and walked away with him.

"Who was that?" Mr. Alden asked.

"We met her in Elmford," Jessie explained.

"She seems like a very nervous lady," Mr. Alden said. But then his mind strayed from Laura Garrison to Benny, who had just dropped his ice cream cone on the street and was looking very surprised.

"Grandfather," Benny shouted. "My

cone! And I hardly had more than four licks."

Grandfather laughed and took Benny's hand. "Don't worry Benny. I'll buy you another one."

For the next few days Jessie tried to forget about the necklace. The children agreed that since they had no more clues to follow, they might as well not think about it. Instead, they continued their planning for Mr. Alden's birthday party.

"I think," Benny said. "we should have a chocolate cake with chocolate icing and chocolate ice cream."

The other children laughed.

"I haven't decided yet what I'm going to play on my violin. I know Grandfather loves waltzes, but I don't know one to play," Violet said.

"I've decided to decorate the dining room with balloons and streamers and especially a big sign that says 'Happy Birthday,' " Jessie said.

"And here is my poem," Henry announced. "It's not very good but at least it's all mine.

"Poems are very hard to write,
And I have tried both day and night.
But this is what I want to say,
Grandfather, have the best birthday."

"I think it's very good," Benny said.
"Me, too," the girls agreed.

They talked more about the party, enjoying all the plans. After dinner, they went up to Henry's room and talked about what they would wear from the attic. Finally, they agreed they were all tired and they wanted to go to bed.

Jessie woke up in the middle of the night and sat up in bed. Was that a noise from downstairs? It was. She just knew it. She got out of bed, quietly opened her door, and looked out.

Henry opened his door at the same time. He knew he had heard sounds from the living room. He looked over toward Jessie's room and saw her standing in the doorway in her white nightgown and bare feet. He tiptoed over to her.

"I heard something," she whispered.

"I did, too," Henry said. "I'm going downstairs."

"Maybe we should get Grandfather," Jessie said.

Henry disagreed. "It could be Watch. How can we wake Grandfather because our dog is walking around?"

Henry started down the stairs. "I'm coming, too," Jessie whispered.

Together they walked down, very slowly, holding hands. They tried to make sure the steps didn't creak. When they got to the bottom, they looked toward the living room. Jessie gasped. A light was moving in the room. Jessie put her arm around Henry's shoulders and they stood still, watching the light glide around the room.

Then, before he knew what he was doing, Henry cried out, "Who's there?" The light

went out and there was silence. "I think we should get Grandfather," Jessie said, sounding frightened.

Henry tiptoed into the room and turned on the light. The room was empty. Suddenly Mr. Alden was coming down the stairs with Violet and Benny behind him.

"What's going on?" he asked when he saw Jessie and Henry.

"We heard some noises, and we saw a light, too," Jessie said. "I think you should call the police."

Grandfather looked around the room. "Nothing has been touched," he said. He went to the desk and took an envelope out of a drawer. He counted the money in it. "There's no money missing either."

"What could it have been, Grandfather?" Jessie asked.

"Well, the noise could have been Watch. And the lights could have come from cars on the road."

Henry said, "Someone could have come in the patio door."

Grandfather looked around again. "Henry, I left my camera on that table. It's still there. Wouldn't a thief have taken it?"

"I guess you're right," Henry said.

Violet eyes opened wide. "Look," she said, pointing to the mantelpiece. "The picture is crooked."

Mr. Alden laughed. "Well, that proves Mrs. McGregor doesn't miss a thing when she dusts."

But the children weren't so sure that's what it meant.

Upstairs, in bed, Jessie pulled her blankets up high, snuggled under them, and hoped that whoever had been in the house wouldn't come back.

CHAPTER 8

Surprise Visits

The next afternoon Aunt Jane appeared. "I just thought I'd drive over to see you. I miss you."

They all sat out on the lawn and the Aldens told their aunt everything that had happened since they had visited her. She listened carefully and then said, "It's very possible none of the things you've told me have anything to do with the necklace. Laura Garrison and Susan may have been talking about something else. And what happened last night could be just what your grandfather said. Lights from the road."

"But the picture was crooked," Jessie protested.

Aunt Jane laughed. "You can't think that every crooked picture in the house means something, dear."

"I just want the necklace back for Grandfather," Jessie said.

"I understand that, but it — " Aunt Jane was interrupted by Mrs. McGregor.

She came out of the house and said to Jessie, "There's a Laura Garrison on the telephone. She said she would like to speak to you."

The children all ran toward the house with Aunt Jane following them. "What do you suppose she wants?" Benny shouted as he ran.

"We'll soon find out," Henry shouted back to him.

When Jessie picked up the phone, she was breathing quickly. "Hello."

"Is this Jessie Alden?" a voice asked.

"Yes," Jessie replied.

"This is Laura Garrison. I'd like to come

to see your grandfather and you children to-night. I want to talk to you."

Jessie couldn't believe it. "Sure," she answered immediately.

"Is eight o'clock all right?" Mrs. Garrison asked.

"I guess that's fine," Jessie said. She hung up the phone. "Mrs. Garrison wants to come over to talk to Grandfather and all of us tonight."

"Wow!" Benny shouted.

"I think I have to stay to meet her," Aunt Jane said. "I'll call Uncle Andy and tell him I'll be here for dinner."

"I wonder what she wants," Henry said.

"Me too," Violet added.

When Mr. Alden came home, Jessie asked him, "Remember that woman we met in the ice cream parlor?"

Mr. Alden nodded.

"Well," Henry said. "She called and said she wants to come to talk to us tonight at eight o'clock."

"What does she want?" Grandfather asked, looking puzzled.

"We're not sure," Violet said.

Mr. Alden turned to Aunt Jane. "Do you know this Mrs. Garrison?"

"No," Aunt Jane said. "But I certainly want to. John, the children will tell you everything soon."

"You are all very mysterious," Mr. Alden said. "But knowing my grandchildren, I guess I'm just going to have to wait until they're good and ready to explain matters to me."

After dinner, the Aldens and Aunt Jane sat in the living room, waiting for Laura Garrison. At 8:15, Mr. Alden said, "Well now, your Mrs. Garrison is late."

At 8:30, Henry said, "Where do you suppose she is?"

And at 9:00, Aunt Jane stood up. "I really don't think she's coming. I'd better get home."

Henry and Jessie walked Aunt Jane to the

door. "What do you think happened? Why do you think she didn't come?" Henry asked.

Aunt Jane shook her head. "I don't know, Henry. This a real mystery to me."

"Maybe something *happened* to her," said Benny, wide-eyed.

Violet laughed. "Oh, Benny, you have such an imagination!"

After Aunt Jane drove off, Jessie said, "Mrs. Garrison wanted to talk about *something*. What?" She didn't try to hide her disappointment.

Henry frowned. "Do you think it was about the necklace?"

"Maybe she'll come tomorrow," Jessie said, hopefully.

"Probably not," Henry said. "We don't seem to be having that much luck with this mystery."

The next morning after breakfast, the Alden children ran down to their boxcar. They sat on the pillows on the floor and Jessie said, "I know Mrs. Garrison isn't going to come today, but I think we could call her and find out why she didn't come here last night."

"How can we call her?" Violet asked. "We don't know her number, or even where she lives."

"Maybe she lives in Elmford," Henry said. "That's where we met her."

"She could just have been visiting there," Benny said. "Like we were visiting Aunt Jane."

"Benny is right," Jessie said. "But Grandfather has a lot of phone books for towns near here in his den. We could try to find her number in one of the books."

The children ran back to Mr. Alden's den and took some telephone books out of the closet. Henry said suddenly, "Often phone numbers are listed under the man's name and we don't even know her husband's first name."

Violet sighed. "I think this whole thing is hopeless."

"Let's just *try*," Jessie said. She took the Elmford phone book and opened it to the

G's. "There are two Garrisons. One is William and one is just listed as L. Maybe the L is her."

Jessie picked up the phone and dialed the number for the L listing. When the ringing was answered, she said, "Is Laura Garrison there?"

A voice on the other end answered, "I'm sorry, you have the wrong number. There is no Laura Garrison here."

"Sorry to bother you," Jessie said, hanging up. She sighed. "Well, that isn't the right number."

"Dial the number for William," Henry said.

Jessie dialed and waited while the phone rang. A young girl answered and Jessie said again. "Is Laura Garrison there?"

"Wrong number," the girl answered and hung up.

Benny said, "Well, she doesn't live in Elmford. This is fun. Where should we try next?"

"What about Kenniston?" Henry said.

Violet said suddenly, "Supposing Mrs. Garrison has an unlisted number."

"What's that?" Benny asked.

Violet turned to Benny. "Well, some people don't want their number listed in the phone book. They want it to be very private. That's an unlisted number."

Jessie shrugged. "Well if it's unlisted, then we'll never find it."

"Okay," Henry said, "let's look in Kenniston."

Violet turned the pages of the Kenniston phone book. "One Garrison. Paul J."

Violet took the phone and dialed the number. It just rang and rang. "No answer," she said.

"Well, that *could* be Laura's number," Jessie said.

"But you don't know for sure," Henry answered.

"Right," Jessie agreed.

"Maybe she is right here in Greenfield," Benny said.

"We'd know if she lived here," Henry said.

"We know just about everybody in Greenfield."

"I think you should look in the phone book," Benny insisted.

Jessie turned the pages of the book. "You're right. There's one Marvin Garrison way out on Cadman Road."

Violet took the phone and dialed the number. "Hello," she said. "Is Laura Garrison there?"

An angry voice replied, "This is the third wrong number I've gotten today. I think I'm just going to disconnect this phone. I've had enough. The last call I had was for the Fairfield Meat Market."

"I'm real sorry," Violet said and she hurriedly hung up.

"I think we should just give up," Henry said.

"Wait a minute," Jessie answered. "We saw her visiting Susan Barstow. Maybe Mrs. Garrison lives in Silver City."

"For all *we* know she could live in New York City," Henry said, smiling.

Jessie turned to the Silver City listings. "There's one. Kenneth Garrison."

Jessie dialed the number and soon a woman answered. "Is Laura Garrison there?" Jessie asked.

"This is Laura Garrison," the woman replied.

Jessie's face broke into a big smile. She put her hand over the receiver and whispered, "It's *her!*"

Then she took her hand away and said to Mrs. Garrison, "This is Jessie Alden. I just wanted to ask you what happened last night. I mean, you didn't come to our house and you'd said you would."

Jessie could hear Laura Garrison sigh. "I'm sorry, Jessie. I should have called you, but I just changed my mind. I really had nothing to say to you after all."

"Please, Mrs. Garrison," Jessie said. "Won't you come and talk to us? I know you wanted to."

"I can't, Jessie. I can't help you. You misunderstood," Mrs. Garrison said.

"You don't have to come to the house," Jessie said quickly. "Just let us talk to you for a few minutes."

Mrs. Garrison hesitated. "All right. I'll meet you at that ice cream parlor in Greenfield in an hour."

Jessie hung up and said in disbelief, "She said to meet her at the ice cream parlor in an hour."

"Now what are you going to do?" Henry asked.

"I don't know." Jessie answered.

"At least we'll get some ice cream, I hope," Benny said.

In an hour the children were at the ice cream shop. Laura Garrison was already there, sitting at a big table, drinking a cup of coffee. The Aldens joined her and she said, "Why don't you all order something."

"I'm not very hungry," Jessie said.

"I am," Benny said quickly.

Laura smiled. "What would you like, Benny?"

"Vanilla ice cream with chocolate fudge sauce," Benny answered.

Henry had a malted, Violet a scoop of chocolate ice cream, and Jessie decided on a soda. As soon as the waitress had taken their order Jessie said, "Mrs. Garrison, we don't mean to be pests, but I just think you wanted to say *something* to us last night. What was it?"

Laura Garrison looked down at her hands. "I made a mistake, Jessie. I thought I had something to tell you that might help you, but I was wrong. That's all, Jessie. I have nothing to say."

The waitress returned with their orders soon and they all started to eat. "If I could help you, I would," Mrs. Garrison said. "But I can't. I think you children just have to forget about the necklace."

"Everybody keeps telling us that," Benny said.

"Well," Laura Garrison answered, "maybe everybody is right."

They all finished their ice cream and then

left the shop. Mrs. Garrison said, "Good-bye children, I don't think we'll be meeting again."

Henry watched her get into her car and drive off. "This is *really* it, Jessie. We've reached the end of the road. I think we do have to forget about the necklace."

"Maybe," Jessie said, but she didn't sound so sure.

The next day, Grandfather and the children were in the kitchen eating a breakfast of Mrs. McGregor's perfect pancakes with real maple syrup, milk for the children, and coffee for Mr. Alden.

The young Aldens walked to the door with their grandfather, so that Jessie, Violet, and Benny could kiss him good-bye before he went to his office. Henry shook hands with Mr. Alden, thinking that he was too grown-up to kiss Grandfather now.

As Mr. Alden was going out to the front door, a car pulled up in the driveway and stopped. A woman and man got out.

When Jessie saw them, she gasped. "Oh! My!"

It was Mrs. Newton and Carl Mason.

Mrs. Newton walked up to the Aldens. "I am sorry to come like this, without calling, and so early. But I knew if I didn't do this right away, I would lose my nerve."

She turned to Mr. Alden. "I'm Lorraine Newton. This is Carl Mason, who is the curator of the Elmford Museum. Your grandchildren know both of us. We would like to talk to all of you."

Grandfather looked very puzzled, but he said politely, "Of course. Won't you please come in."

In the living room, Mr. Alden asked his guests, "Would you like some coffee or something to eat, perhaps?"

"No, thank you very much," Mrs. Newton answered. She reached into her large handbag, took out a velvet jewelry box, and handed it to Mr. Alden. "I think this belongs to you."

Grandfather opened the box and gasped.

There was the sapphire necklace, sparkling against a white satin background. He looked at Mrs. Newton. "It's my wife's necklace. But I don't understand. How did you get it?"

Mrs. Newton sighed. "This is a long story. But before I begin I must say that I am very sorry for what I have done . . . for all the pain I must have caused you and your wife."

"Please, tell us your story, Mrs. Newton," Mr. Alden said.

She nodded. "I had a son, Evan Newton. He really wasn't a bad person, but he was lazy. He was married and had two children, and they all lived with my husband and myself, because Evan just didn't want to work.

"Finally, after a few years of this, my husband told Evan he wasn't going to give him any more money. Evan *had* to get a job. Well, he did, with a caterer."

"Oh!" Violet said.

Mrs. Newton went on. "Not long after he got the job, he left it, bragging that he was going to have enough money soon to do all sorts of things. I was very suspicious. One day, when Evan was out, I went up to his room, looking for some explanation of his attitude. In his drawer, under a pile of shirts, I found the necklace."

"I can hardly believe this," Mr Alden cried out.

Mrs. Newton, twisting her hands in her lap, went on. "I was very upset. I asked Evan where he had gotten the necklace and he wouldn't tell me. My husband and I kept asking him, but he would never answer. I never read anything about a theft of a necklace in any newspaper. We waited for weeks, trying to find something out. I *wanted* to return it."

"Why didn't you go to the police?" Henry asked.

Mrs. Newton wiped away a tear. "I should have, but Evan was my son and I couldn't stand the thought of his going to jail. And then there were his children. How would they feel about a father who was a thief?

Susan, Evan's wife, begged me not to tell the police."

"So you didn't," Grandfather said, nodding his head.

"I didn't," Mrs. Newton said. "But I didn't want to keep the necklace, either. So I donated it to the Elmford Museum. I felt, in that way, I wouldn't be keeping the necklace and lots of people would be able to enjoy looking at it in the museum. I told Mr. Mason the whole story and he took the necklace even though he was reluctant."

"I know I shouldn't have done that," Carl Mason said. "I thought about what to do for days. I knew I should go to the police, but Mrs. Newton was a dear, old friend. I felt sorry for her."

"Where is Evan now?" Violet asked.

"Evan died a number of years ago," Mrs. Newton answered. "Then his wife married John Barstow and they moved to Silver City, where Evan's children grew up. I wanted to forget about the necklace, but recently, Mr. Alden, your grandchildren came to Elmford and went to see Elizabeth Harkins."

"Why did you all do that?" Grandfather asked Jessie.

The children told him the story of seeing Mrs. Harkins' picture and everything that happened after that.

Mrs. Newton said, "Elizabeth and her husband are old friends. They were the only people I told about Evan and the necklace, except, of course, for Carl. So the Harkinses called and told me about the children's visit to her."

Henry turned to Mr. Mason. "*You* threw away Violet's drawing, didn't you?"

"Yes," Mr. Mason admitted. "I did. I thought you children would give it up. But you didn't."

"And I made the call to your aunt's, telling you to go home," Mrs. Newton said. "It was so wrong to do that."

"Did you follow us in your car, Mr. Mason?" Benny asked. "You scared me."

Mr. Mason smiled. "I'm sorry, Benny. I just wanted to see if you were all going to

Mrs. Newton's that day. When I saw you weren't, I drove away."

Violet said, "We knew, we *really* knew it was our grandmother's necklace."

Mrs. Newton twisted a handkerchief in her hands. "Laura wanted to tell you all along. In fact, when she made that appointment to come here the night before last, it was to tell all of you the whole truth. But I found out and I couldn't let her do it. So I persuaded her not to come.

"Susan Barstow wanted to keep the truth hidden, too. She just couldn't face telling her children what their father had done. She told me about your visit to her house. She felt very bad about the way she acted, but she didn't know what else to do."

Henry stood up and faced Mr. Mason. "Were Jessie and I right? Was someone here the other night?"

Mr. Mason sighed. "I'm sorry. *I* was here that night. All I wanted to do was look at the portrait. I *had* to see if the children's story was true. As soon as I saw the necklace I knew, Mr. Alden, it was yours. I can't tell you how guilty I feel for having broken in here. It was wrong for me to have done that and I apologize."

"How did you get in?" Mr. Alden asked.

Carl Mason smiled. "Well, the lock on your patio door can be opened very easily. You should have it looked at. I am very sorry if I frightened you."

"What did you do after you were here that night?" Jessie asked.

"I called Mrs. Newton right away, even though it was the middle of the night, and told her that the necklace was Mr. Alden's. Then she said she would have to return it to him, no matter what."

Mr. Alden opened the jewelry box again and looked at the glittering sapphires. "How happy Celia would be if she knew it was back!"

Mrs. Newton stood up. "I'll leave you now. I could never apologize enough for what I have done all these years."

Mr. Alden stood, too. "I understand what

you felt . . . that you wanted to protect your son. You don't have to worry. My grandchildren and I will never let anyone know that Evan was the thief. I have Celia's necklace, and that's all that matters. Your son is dead. There is really nothing to be gained by reporting this matter to the police at this time."

"Thank you, Mr. Alden," Mrs. Newton said. Then she turned to the children, "And thank all of you for not giving up looking for the truth."

Then she and Carl Mason left.

The children all gathered around Mr. Alden and looked at the necklace. Mr. Alden handed the box to Jessie. "I told you once that this was to be given to the oldest granddaughter. Well, that's you, Jessie."

"You're rich, Jessie!" Benny cried.

Jessie gazed at the necklace for a long moment. Then she closed the box. "Grandfather, would you mind if I gave it back to the museum?"

"Why, Jessie?" Grandfather asked.

Jessie answered, "Well, I'm too young to wear it now. So what would we do with it?"

"I'd put it in the safe," Grandfather said.

Jessie nodded and said, "And no one would see it. But if I gave it to the Elmford Museum, people could come and enjoy our beautiful necklace. I'd like that."

Grandfather smiled at Jessie. "You are a very generous, thoughtful girl. Of course, if that's what you want, that's what we'll do."

Benny shook his head. "But, Jessie, it's *yours*."

"I know, Benny," Jessie said, "and that's why I can give it to the museum."

CHAPTER 9

Happy Endings

The next morning, Grandfather and the Alden children drove to the Elmford Museum. Mr. Mason looked up as they all walked into his office.

"My granddaughter has something to say to you, Mr. Mason," Mr. Alden said.

Mr. Mason looked very nervous. "Oh," he said.

Jessie wet her lips. "Mr. Mason, I've decided that I want to give my necklace to your museum."

"You *do*?" Mr. Mason cried out. "How wonderful! But are you sure?"

Jessie nodded. "I'm sure," she said as she handed him the jewelry box. Mr. Mason put an arm around her shoulder. "Let's all put it back into its case."

They walked to the little room that had held the necklace. Mr. Mason opened the display case and put the necklace in it. The six of them stood and admired its beauty.

Suddenly, Mr. Mason, said, "Just one minute. I'll be right back." He left the room and returned five minutes later. He had a small card in his hand that he slid into a yellow window below the necklace.

Jessie bent over and read aloud, "Donated by Miss Jessie Alden."

"Wow!" Benny said. "You're famous now, Jessie."

Mr. Mason smiled. "Jessie, when you get older, anytime you want to wear the necklace . . . to a dance or a very fancy party, whatever, you just call me."

Jessie smiled. "I'd like that."

Mr. Mason turned to Violet. "You draw very well, young lady. Don't stop."

Violet grinned. "Thank you!"

Then the Aldens left.

The ride home was a happy one. They were all excited by the events of the morning.

Jessie said to Violet, "You know, you can borrow the necklace anytime, too."

Violet laughed. "I'll wear it to my first real grown-up dance or party."

As soon as the car pulled into the Alden's driveway, the children ran to the boxcar. The word "party" had made them all think of the same thing . . . Grandfather's birthday.

"It's only a week away," Henry said.

"We have a lot to do," Benny said.

"Let's go up to the attic and pick out what we are going to wear," Jessie said.

Henry and Benny both frowned. "Are you sure we should do this?"

"Of course," Violet insisted. "It will be fun."

They went up to the attic and started going through trunks and closets. Henry decided to wear the velvet coat he had found before.

Violet wanted the lavender hat and she found a long white dress to wear with it. Jessie held up a blue chiffon dress that reached the floor. "I like this one," she said.

"Think of how lovely your necklace would look with that," Violet said.

Benny found an old child's sailor suit and complained when his sisters made him put it on.

"You look wonderful," Jessie said. "Grandfather will love it."

But Henry covered his mouth with his hand, so Benny wouldn't see him laughing.

"I'm only wearing it for Grandfather," Benny said. "I think it looks silly."

The next day the Aldens went to Barlow's Men's Shop and looked at sweaters for Mr. Alden's gift. Benny wanted to buy a bright red one. Violet wanted a blue one. Jessie loved a green sweater. Henry finally said, "Let's buy one that *Grandfather* would want, not one we'd like for ourselves."

They all had to agree that the gray wool was what Grandfather would like the best.

When they reached home, they went up to Violet's room and she wrapped the sweater in gift paper. She had made her own card and they all signed it. When she made a big bow for the top of the gift box, Benny said, "Violet, you're the best wrapper in the world."

They had planned the party as a surprise dinner party and had invited Aunt Jane and Uncle Andy. The morning of Mr. Alden's birthday, the children all pretended to sleep late, so that Grandfather would go to his office before seeing them. They wanted to give him his present at the dinner party.

That day, Mrs. McGregor made Mr. Alden's favorite dinner . . . fried chicken, mashed potatoes, green beans, and a big salad. All the children helped make the chocolate cake. Violet decorated it very carefully. When the cake was finished, Jessie decorated the dining room and living room with bal-

loons. Then she hung streamers around the portrait of their grandmother. Violet practiced the Blue Danube waltz, which she had decided to play on her violin. Aunt Jane and Uncle Andy arrived at five o'clock, and everyone was waiting when Mr. Alden came home at five-thirty.

The children all had on their clothes from the attic and they shouted "Surprise!" as Grandfather came into the balloon-filled living room. A big sign on the doorway read HAPPY BIRTHDAY!

Grandfather laughed out loud when he saw the children. "Where did you get those clothes?" he asked.

"From your very own attic," Benny answered.

Grandfather said to Benny, "You are wearing your great-grandfather's sailor suit."

"Really," Benny said. "I didn't even know I had a great-grandfather."

Mr. Alden opened his present from the children, and even though it was a warm evening, he put the sweater on for a little while. Aunt Jane and Uncle Andy gave him a book he had wanted.

Then they all went into the living room and enjoyed every bite of Mrs. McGregor's wonderful meal. When she came in carrying the cake everyone sang "Happy Birthday." Watch barked along with the song.

Violet played her violin piece and Henry recited his poem. Just then the doorbell rang. Aunt Jane and Uncle Andy looked at each other slyly. Mrs. McGregor answered the door and came back with Mrs. Newton, who was carrying an armful of roses. "I always seem to be visiting you uninvited. But Aunt Jane told me it was your birthday, Mr. Alden. I wanted to bring these flowers to put on the mantelpiece next to your wife's picture. They are my own prize-winning roses, which I grow in my yard. I though they would look very pretty with the portrait."

The whole family went into the living room. Jessie got a vase filled with water and they placed the roses next to the portrait.

Grandfather smiled. "This is one of the best parties I've ever had."

He looked at the portrait. "And do you know what one of the best presents I've ever gotten is?"

"What, Grandfather?" Violet asked.

"It's knowing," Grandfather said, "that your grandmother's necklace is safe and sound. I thank you children for that."

"Aunt Jane helped, too," Benny said.

Grandfather turned to his sister and said, "I thank you, too, Jane."

Jane smiled. "It really was the children, not me. They just wouldn't give up. I told them they took after you."

Violet said shyly, "There is no better person to take after."

One by one they went over to their grandfather and kissed him. Even Henry forgot about trying to be grown-up and kissed his grandfather.

Jessie looked at the necklace in the portrait and said, "I think it is sparkling more now than any other time."

"That's because it's Grandfather's birthday," Benny said.

"I think he's right," Mrs. Newton said.

They all laughed and turned to Grandfather who was looking at his wife's portrait with love. "Thank you, all," he said.

GERTRUDE CHANDLER WARNER discovered when she was teaching that many readers who like an exciting story could find no books that were both easy and fun to read. She decided to try to meet this need, and her first book, *The Boxcar Children*, quickly proved she had succeeded.

Miss Warner drew on her own experiences to write the mystery. As a child she spent hours watching trains go by on the tracks opposite her family home. She often dreamed about what it would be like to set up housekeeping in a caboose or freight car — the situation the Alden children find themselves in.

When Miss Warner received requests for more adventures involving Henry, Jessie, Violet, and Benny Alden, she began additional stories. In each, she chose a special setting and introduced unusual or eccentric characters who like the unpredictable.

While the mystery element is central to each of Miss Warner's books, she never thought of them as strictly juvenile mysteries. She liked to stress the Aldens' independence and resourcefulness and their solid New England devotion to using up and making do. The Aldens go about most of their adventures with as little adult supervision as possible — something else that delights young readers.

Miss Warner lived in Putnam, Connecticut, until her death in 1979. During her lifetime, she received hundreds of letters from girls and boys telling her how much they liked her books.